A Love Tucked Away in the Attic

A Love Tucked Away in the Attic

By Heather Marie Roberson

To all who believed in me

Chapter One

The rain was pounding on the roof of the attic. Thunder was loud as it rolled across the sky. The musty smell from mothballs and old junk engulfed the air as the dust tickled my nose. Spider webs dressed an old mannequin and an empty bookshelf. Grandma Daisy stood in a corner going through boxes labeled *Helen's baby clothes.* My little sister was in the corner giggling as she tried on old dresses from a trunk and danced around in front of a mirror. I was moving boxes labeled *fancy china* closer to Grandma Daisy, trying my best not to slip on my own sweat.

On the hottest day of summer vacation, my mom decided my chore for the day was to babysit my five year old sister and help my grandma go through the things in her attic. I'm only fifteen years old. I shouldn't need to make adult decisions like what life memorabilia Grandma Daisy should throw away or keep when she moves into our house tomorrow.

"What are you going to do with all this stuff, Grandma Daisy?" I asked as I set the box down, relieved I didn't drop it.

"Oh, I suspect your parents will take some of it. Maybe your aunts will want some. Most I'm sure will be taken over to St. Vinnies or Goodwill," Grandma replied as she opened the box.

"Why would anyone want this junk Grandma Daisy? It's all dusty, smelly, out of style and just plain old. Well, except for this lace dress," Hattie said, holding up a lace wedding dress about six sizes too big for her. The years in the trunk had stained it yellow. "Oh, Grandma Daisy, could you make me some dresses with this old thing for my baby dolls or maybe a summer dress for me?"

"Oh, heavens child, no," Grandma exclaimed taking it from her and holding it up against herself, gazing in the mirror looking lost in thought. "This was my wedding dress. Many many years ago."

"Wow you use to be skinny Grandma Daisy. It wouldn't fit you now. Please make me a dress. Please, Grandma Daisy, Please." Hattie whined.

I bent down and started rummaging through the trunk. The rain started coming down harder on the roof. A loud clap of thunder shook the house making the dim attic lights flicker. My fingers came across some envelopes wrapped in a large white cloth handkerchief, with four blueberries embroidered on it. As I was taking a letter out of one of the envelopes, I noticed a couple of black and white pictures sticking out of one of the envelopes.

"Grandma Daisy is this you and Grandpa? You guys were so young."

She took the pictures from me and sat in the old rocking chair under the light. The attic floor creaked as my grandma rocked back and forth. For a second time in a matter of minutes, she looked lost in thought.

"Will you tell us about Grandpa?" I asked as I pulled out a quilt and a couple throw pillows from another trunk nearby. As I started to spread the musty patchwork quilt out on the attic floor, a memory came floating to me of when I was younger. Grandpa was spreading the blanket out under the dining room table on a rainy day. Him and I would get under the table and arrange pillows while Grandma Daisy would slide a tray of fresh baked chocolate chip cookies under the table for us to eat.

"Are you ready for a story?" Grandpa would ask. He would finger his chin of white whiskers while he thumbed through an old picture book as I would scream in my little girl voice "YES!"

"Oh not that old story again," Grandma Daisy would laugh. "She probably has that one memorized by now. Why don't you tell her the story of when her mother was in the parade?" she would say, grabbing the picture book from Grandpa as she made herself comfortable under the table with us.

A loud clap of thunder brings me back to reality. I catch a picture as it slid off Grandma Daisy's lap down her blue polyester pants. I glance at it closer this time. Grandma had the biggest and brightest smile in the picture, and a twinkle in her eye. She was holding a stuffed bear and a stick cotton candy. A man stood behind her with his arms around her waist. He was a sailor in uniform. His head was turned facing her, but you could see he was smiling from ear to ear. Grandpa was never in the Navy. Not that I could remember anyway. I had heard plenty of stories of Grandpa, but never any military stories of him.

In the other picture, all the ladies had on these 1940's era floral dresses that buttoned from top to bottom with belts that hugged their waist. Their hair was so elegantly pulled back with curls that hung below their ears. A lady at the end of the row had on an oversized brim hat with a tiny bow tied around the crown of the hat. Then I recognize my grandma's brother. My mom's Uncle John. He and some of the guys had on long baggy pants with creases down the middle. Two wore suspenders over a button up shirt and two wore belts. And then there was the sailor again, sitting next to Grandma with his arm over her shoulder.

I hand Grandma the pictures, "Grandma Daisy, who is that sailor with you in these pictures? It's not Grandpa is it?" She takes the pictures from me. I see her take a finger and trace the sailor's face. She smiles but with sadness in her eyes she tells Hattie and I, "No that's not your grandpa. His name was William Barret."

"Well who is he?" Hattie and I ask in unison.

"William Barret was ...Well he was my first true love."

Chapter Two

"Oh Grandma Daisy, tell us about William. You know I love romantic stories."

Grandma took her eyes from the picture and looked at me and said, "Hanna, do you remember when you told me about you and your friend Nash?"

"Yes, I remember."

"Well, how did you feel when he finally asked you to be his girlfriend? How did you feel every time you were together?"

I felt a smile come across my lips as I thought about Nash, "I was nervous and excited all at the same time Grandma Daisy. Every time he would call, my heart would start racing. I would have to control my breathing so I wouldn't sound weird over the phone. I would be so nervous and hoped my hands weren't sweaty in case he would try to hold it. And then I remember my stomach feeling like it was full of butterflies the first time we kissed. I was so happy." I paused for a moment remembering that day. It was only a couple of weeks ago, "Oh Grandma Daisy, being in love is so...well, it's magical, wonderful, scary, and exciting all at the same time. I never want it to end."

"Well, my child," Grandma Daisy replied with a smile as she stroked my hair, "That is how I felt the few short days William and I shared together. I can remember those days like it was yesterday." Then my grandma began to tell us all about William.

"I was living in California then. I was barely seventeen years old when we met. He and some other sailors fresh out of boot camp were enjoying their last bit of freedom before heading across the Pacific to do their part in WWII. My brother John was dating my best friend Patricia. There was a dance one night down at the town hall. Momma let me tag along with John and Patricia, mostly just to keep an eye on them. Momma thought they might be getting a little too frisky with each other. However, like any good best friend, I kept my nose out of Patricia's business when I saw her and John sneak away to the kissing closet. I was standing over by the punch table with my other two best friends, Mary and Sue-Ellen, when I felt a tap on my shoulder. "Excuse, me Miss, could I have this dance?"

All I could do was stare. He had the greenest eyes I had ever seen. When he smiled his eyes twinkled. His skin was tan, and he smelled of aftershave. Standing there in his dress whites, he was the most handsome boy I had ever laid my eyes on. Mary snapped me back to reality when she whispered," What are you waiting for Daisy? Go danoo with him." She took the punch out of my hand and Sue-Ellen pushed me closer to the sailor. I cleared my throat as politely as I could and I accepted his hand as he led me to the dance floor.

The band was playing some fast jazz music. William led me all over the dance floor. It was exhilarating, even though I had two left feet. He of course, reminded me of Fred Astaire. By the time the music ended I was laughing hard and trying to catch my breath. He grabbed punch for both of us and we went outside to cool down. There was a slight breeze in the night air, but it felt good after being in the stuffy building. We sat on the swings and sipped our punch.

"So, what's your name sailor?" I asked breaking the awkward silence.

"I'm William Barret." he replied, extending his hand for me to shake, "And your name is?"

"I'm Gwendolyn, but everyone calls me Daisy" I answered, accepting his hand. My heart skipped a beat when William raised it to his lips and kissed my hand like a gentleman. I could feel goosebumps crawl up my arms

"It's a pleasure to meet you, Daisy."

"Likewise, William. So, where are you from?" I asked, looking down at my feet. I didn't want him to notice how he made me blush.

"The Midwest, "William replied, "How about you?'

"I'm from here, silly. Born and raised," I laughed. "Where did you learn to dance like that?"

"We have dances like this back home. When I was younger, I'd watch the adults dance all the time. Then I'd go home and practice. My sister was a great dance partner. She and I won the church talent show a couple of years back."

"Oh, wow! That's amazing. How long will you be in town? Maybe you could teach me. If you didn't notice, I have two left feet." He wouldn't have to teach me. I just really wanted to be able to hold him close and smell his intoxicating scent again.

"I fly out on Tuesday to meet up with the USS Essex. But everyone says the war is almost over. I pray every night that it ends before I get over there. A lot of boys I went to school with have already lost their lives. Their families are devastated. I don't want my family going through that heartache." The moonlight shone bright enough that I could see the sadness in his eyes.

"My dad says I need to man up. This war is my right of passage. Kick some Japanese ass, and I'll be a man. If I die, I die a hero." He sighed and took a long drink of his punch.

My heart ached for William. I couldn't imagine doing something that would put your life in danger. I didn't know what to do or say. But suddenly I found myself grabbing his hand. It was warm and soft. Definitely not the hand of a farmer. My heart started to beat really fast. William looked at me and smiled.

"So how did you acquire the nickname Daisy?" He asked with curiosity in his voice.

"My momma said she gave me that nickname shortly after I was born. She said one look at me and she could tell I was beautiful, pure, and innocent, just like the daisies growing in the garden. Momma also told me the word daisy comes from the old English word ' Daes eag,' which means 'day's eye' because they always have their petals open at the crack of dawn. Momma said I was always wide awake and chipper at the crack of dawn." I laughed at that thought, then finished, "I guess I'm still that way."

"Wow! That is quite interesting. I guess one learns something new every day huh? William said, "Now every time I see a daisy I will think of you. Although, you are far more beautiful than a daisy." he replied as he took his finger and slid it from the bottom of my ear to my chin, again making me blush. I could hear the music start up again inside.

"Um..let's go dance again," I said, grabbing his hand and leading him towards the building.

Kids swarmed the dance floor. Music resonated from the saxophones and trumpets. Swing music was sweeping the nation, and if you couldn't jump and jive, than you might as well just sit. And that is what I wanted to do. "Just let me lead, okay?" William whispered in my ear. Like before, he had me all over the dance floor. Only this time I felt more comfortable. I didn't worry about my two left feet. Or the fact that I was dancing with the most adorable sailor in the United States Navy.

When the song ended Sue-Ellen and Mary came skipping up to William and I. Full of giggles, they introduced themselves, "HI I'm Sue-Ellen. My, aren't you two a great looking couple?"

"And I'm Mary. Where did you learn to dance like that? "

William was making small talk with the girls when the leader of the band announced, "Alright fellas, grab your best girl. We are going to slow it down one last time and then call it a night. Thank you all for coming out tonight. And boys, we look forward to seeing you all come home soon."

"Excuse me, ladies," William said, "Daisy, may I have this last dance?" He held out his hand and I graciously accepted. We strolled onto the dance floor as Mary and Sue-Ellen giggled and whispered. William wrapped his arm around my waist and pulled me close. I could hear his heart beating as I rested my head on his chest. We slowly swayed to the rhythm of the music with the rest of the couples on the dance floor.

I inhaled the smell of his aftershave. I had to make a memory. From this moment on I knew every time I heard Ella Fitzgerald and Louis Armstrong's version of *Dream a Little Dream of Me*, I would think of William and this perfect moment.

After the song ended people were making their way out to their cars. I saw my brother and Patricia standing around chatting with a group of kids. With my hand still intertwined with William's, I dragged him over to where my brother was. The crowd of guys welcomed him right away and started asking him all kinds of questions about the war. He didn't even get the chance to tell them he was deploying for the first time in a couple days because someone came around with a camera and told us all to squeeze together. William and I sat on the bench. As Patricia and some girls sat next to us, William put his arm around me. John and his friends stood behind us. "Looks like someone has a crush on you," John whispered, right before the flash came.

   "Would you mind if I walked your sister home?" William asked John after the picture. John shook his hand and said, "Sure, just don't let my Mom and Dad see you two. Dad doesn't want Daisy to have any dates until she is eighteen." And then John and Patricia walked out the door hand in hand.

William and I walked out into the cool night air. The moonlight guided our way as we walked through the park. "So, um, I know one should never ask a lady her age, but if your dad doesn't want you to have any dates until you turn eighteen well, um ." he stammered.

"I'm not as young as you may be thinking," I huffed, crossing my arms over my chest, "I just turned seventeen. And I have had a boyfriend before. I just made sure my dad never found out. How old are you?"

"Hold on, don't go getting all upset. It was just a question." He remarked as he gently grabbed my elbow. "I just turned eighteen. Hey, if your brother is eighteen, how come he didn't get drafted like the rest of us?"

"If you watch him walk, you would see that he has a limp. He is supposed to walk with a cane but he's too proud and he wants

Patricia to think he is tough. But Patricia and I have been best friends since we were three years old. She was there the day he fell out of the tree. She knows everything about me and my family. With his injury, John wouldn't be useful on a ship or in the infantry. Instead, he helps out at the hospital over on the base. Mom and Patricia are terrified that an opportunity will come up for him to fight. He wants to go over and get those Japs so badly."

William was silent for a minute then asked," So, do you work after school or do anything for fun?"

"Well, I'm the second born out of five kids. Momma makes me come right home after school and help with my younger siblings and in the kitchen. Once they are all in bed, that's when I have to do my studies. Mondays and Thursdays I do get a break from home. I help out at the public library. I don't get paid much, but I save most everything I make. Someday I would love to further my education and become a teacher." Then I looked up and realized where we were. I sighed. "That's my house down at the corner," I said quietly.

William looked in the direction of my house and sighed too, "I had a lot of fun dancing with someone who has two left feet," he laughed, "Hey, do you think you'd be able to sneak away tomorrow? I have liberty starting at seventeen hundred hours. There is fair at the fairgrounds right outside of base."

Of course at that moment I started to giggle like my friends had at the dance early in the night. I bit my lower lip to try to hold my excitement in. "Well, if I knew what seventeen hundred hours meant, I could give you an answer."

William laughed "Living in a military town, I thought you'd know. My apologies," he said as he bowed the way gentlemen do.

"Would you be as kind as to meet me by the cotton candy booth at five o'clock tomorrow night Miss. Daisy?"

I curtsied and replied, "It would be my pleasure, Mr. Barret." Then William took both of my hands and pulled me closer to him. He ever so sweetly kissed me on my cheek and then whispered in my ear, "Good night Gwendolyn, the most beautiful daisy in the garden." I was frozen to my spot. I couldn't stop smiling as he walked away in the opposite direction. Then all of a sudden, I broke out into laughter as I saw him take a running start and jump, kicking his heels together like a happy leprechaun.

Chapter Three

Grandma Daisy paused from her story when she heard a voice coming from downstairs. "Mom? Girls? Are you up there?" It was my mom climbing up the retractable stairs to the attic. "Mom, how on earth did you get up here?"

"For heaven sakes, Helen. I'm not as old as you think I am." Grandma scolded as she slowly made her way out of the rocking chair. "One is only as old as she feels."

Mom shook her head. "I'm serious, Mom. You don't want to overdo it in your condition." she argued as she climbed the last step and entered the attic. She put her hands on her hips and looked around. "Did you ladies get all these boxes sorted? The Goodwill truck will be here tomorrow morning."

"Grandma was telling us a story about William," Hattie said as she made her way off the blanket and into Mom's arms. "Who was your first true love mom?"

Mom took the pictures out of Hattie's hand and looked at them. "William? I thought Daddy was your first true love," Mom smiled, "It's a little warm up here, Mom. Why don't we all go down stairs? It has cooled off since it stopped raining so I opened up your windows to let in some cool fresh air. Besides, it's time for Hattie's nap. I'll lay her down on your bed. Okay, Mom? And Hanna there are boxes in Grandma's kitchen. Take them out to my van, please."

Mom was right. It felt twenty degrees cooler down stairs then in the attic. A nice breeze was coming in through the windows, making my grandma's white lace curtains dance around. As I walked into the kitchen, I started to notice how empty Grandma Daisy's house was becoming. Boxes were neatly stacked against the wall and carefully labeled. No doubt my mom and aunts had been quite busy. Cabinets were open signaling they were empty. Furniture was labeled with brightly colored sticky notes. Each color representing which family member it was going to. It was a little overwhelming to see my grandma's house like this and then to know that by the end of the week it would be empty. No sign that Grandma Daisy and Grandpa ever lived here. No sign that my mom and aunts and uncles grew up here. No sign of me sitting underneath the table listening to Grandpa's stories. No sign of all the cousins playing in the backyard during family gatherings. Soon there would be no sign my family ever occupied this house. The only thing left will be the memories we will carry in our hearts.

As I grabbed the boxes Mom had asked me to grab and took them out to the van, I made a mental note to ask Grandma Daisy if I could have the patchwork quilt and the envelope of pictures and the letters wrapped in the handkerchief.. All the other family members were getting special things from Grandma Daisy, so why shouldn't I? Besides, special black and white pictures shouldn't be thrown out or sold in the thrift stores. What person would want pictures of strangers? I love hearing stories about my great grandparents and their families. Such grand adventures they had, though they probably wouldn't think so. There was a lot of hardship when it came to emigrating from another country all the way to America.

When I came back inside, Mom was helping Grandma Daisy with her medication and asking if she'd like to officially come to our house now or have one last night in her home. "Oh, please Grandma Daisy, one last night here. I'll stay with you. You can finish telling me the story of William. Please, Mom can I stay here too," I begged.

After seeing the smile on my grandma's face and hearing the excitement in my voice she couldn't say no. "Oh I suppose. But no wild parties. Tomorrow is a big day." Then she continued to go through the huge checklist she compiled of who was coming at what time tomorrow. Who was loading and unloading the moving truck. What time the final walk through would be the day after that. And on top of that, we had to find time for school shopping for Hattie and myself. What a way to end the summer. But at least mom had talked my Grandma Daisy into living at our house instead of some fancy overpriced retirement home my aunt and uncles were trying to get her to move into an hour away.

Mom, Dad, Aunt Ginny, and Uncle Roger spent the rest of the afternoon bringing the boxes down from the attic. I was overjoyed that Grandma Daisy let me have the pictures, letters, and the patchwork quilt. Then we ladies finished what was left of the packing, and I had to clean the bathrooms and vacuum the upstairs bedrooms. The sun eventually came back out and dried the grass. Dad and Uncle Roger mowed the yard and trimmed the bushes and cleaned out the flower beds one last time. Since all of Grandma Daisy's things were packed away in the kitchen, and Mom and Aunt Ginny didn't feel like cooking at their houses, we went into town and ate dinner at Grandma's favorite little streetcar diner.

The diner was small. So small that everyone in it heard the stories my family shared over supper. Some of the stories were so funny that all the staff took a break and sat and listened. Some of the staff even shared memories of my family. I guess that is what happens in a small town. It was good to see my grandma laugh and smile. Heck, it was good to see all my family laugh and smile. Ever since the decision had been made that it was best for my grandma to move out of her big house, there had been some tense moments between my parents and aunts and uncles. I understood why they argued over fine china, furniture, and other sentimental items. But Grandma Daisy and Grandpa had saved so many things over the years, I didn't understand why all of it couldn't be distributed evenly between everyone.

Chapter Four

It was about eight-thirty when my parents dropped Grandma Daisy and I off at her house. "Remember, no party girls. We have a busy day tomorrow," my mom yelled from the car window as my dad drove off.

As the sun set, it cast a nice hue of pinks and purples across the horizon. The evening air was perfect for the families who decided to take late night bike rides down quite Hudson Avenue. Small flashes of light came from the grass as the lightning bugs made their presence known.

"Grandma Daisy, could we sit out on the porch and you finish telling me the story of William Barret?" I asked.

"I don't see why not. Be a dear and get me a glass of water first so I can take my medicine." she instructed

I ran inside and ran upstairs to grab the patchwork quilt and the pictures. Then I raced down the steps and into the kitchen. Luckily, the box of cups and glasses were easy to find. I filled the cup with water and grabbed the pills from the counter and headed outside.

Grandma Daisy was sitting in a white wicker rocking chair whistling a tune I couldn't make out. I made myself comfortable on the porch swing as she swallowed her pills. I stared out into the yard and watched the lightening bugs flicker. Then I saw my grandma's flowers and saw the daisies growing tall among the other flowers in her garden. Then I remembered something from earlier. "Grandma Daisy, did Great Grandma Lucille really call you Daisy because she thought you were pure and innocent and you liked to wake up early in the morning?"

"She sure did. Many years ago before she passed away, Grandpa Harry and I dug a lot of those daisies out of her garden and transplanted them right over there."

"You mean those daisies are over one hundred years old?" I asked bewildered.

Grandma Daisy laughed. "The daisy roots are buried deep and are strong. Just like our family is. But new daisies come up every year. Just like you have new cousins born every couple of years. Our family keeps growing and passing on strong rooted values."

"Grandma Daisy, why did Mom think your first true love was Grandpa Harry?"

Grandma Daisy sat silent for a minute lost in thought, "Honey, to be honest, I am not sure I ever told your mother or your aunts and uncles. It wasn't that I didn't want to. After they were born, life became busy for your grandpa and myself and eventually, the memories of William became tucked away, until now that is." She paused for a minute. "Now, how old are you again, Hanna?"

"I'm fifteen, Grandma Daisy."

"Okay, good. I believe you are old enough to hear this next part," she said.

I gave her my one raised eyebrow look. "Wow, Grandma Daisy, this must be serious."

"Alright, child. Now let's continue on with the story, shall we?" And so Grandma Daisy began with her sneaking off to the fair.

"Now I told Sue-Ellen everything that had happened after the dance with William and me.

She, of course, turned into one of those giggly girls. I knew Daddy would never let me go to the fair with William, so Sue-Ellen promised she would cover for me. I would tell my parents I was over at Sue-Ellen's house working on a school project. But I had to promise to be home no later than nine o'clock that night. Sue-Ellen had to be in bed at nine and couldn't promise she could cover for me from her bed.

William was already at the cotton candy booth when I arrived. I almost didn't recognize him in his uniform. There were so many sailors there. They all looked the same, dressed in their nicely creased white uniforms. He ran over and picked me up and spun me around. My legs shot out and I almost kicked someone. "I was wondering if you were going to come."

"Of course I was coming. I wouldn't miss our first date for the world." I said laughing. "So what should we do first?"

There was so much to do. There were booths with games such as throwing a baseball and knocking down pins. There was a booth with little guns you could use to shoot cowboys and bandits. All had prizes to win. There was a booth full of church ladies selling jams and baked goods. There was a booth for fried food that smelled so delicious, you could get full just sniffing the air. And there was a Ferris wheel, a photo booth, and a stage where a band was getting set up to play. Kids were running from one thing to another, while adults gathered around picnic tables catching up on town gossip.

"How about I win you one of those teddy bears?" He said as he guided me over to the baseball throwing game.

He only had to throw the ball once and he knocked down all the pins. The man behind the booth handed me a small brown teddy bear holding a heart.

"Okay, my turn." I smiled and pushed William out of the way. The man behind the booth set the pins back up and placed three small balls in front of me. I only needed one as I also knocked all the pins down on my first throw.

I noticed William staring at me almost in shock. I just smiled as the man behind the booth handed me another brown teddy bear holding a heart. "My brother and I sometimes throw the ball around if we have nothing else going on," I said as I handed the second teddy bear to him. "Now we will have something to remember each other by when you deploy."

"How about we try not to think about the fact that I'm leaving in two days." William laughed as he grabbed my hand and we headed off to the next game booth. For a good hour, we laughed as we played games and ate fried doughnuts. He bought a small bucket of popcorn and we ended up running around the fairgrounds throwing popcorn at each other. Then we bought a ticket to ride the Ferris wheel. As we started going up, William put his arm around me. I snuggled up against his shoulder. No one said a word. Just silence between us. I don't think we even heard the music coming from the band below. When our seat reached the top, it felt like we were on top of the world. The giant ships that were docked on base looked like toys my little brothers played with in the bathtub. It would only be a matter of time before those ships left to relieve the ships that were fighting the battles in the Pacific.

I lifted my head and looked at William. His eyes were sad. He looked at me and smiled. "Let's try not to think about it okay." He said as if he was reading my mind. I knew he was scared. Young and scared and needing to impress his father.

When we got off the Ferris wheel I asked, "If you could do anything and I mean anything right now, what would it be."

"Live my life to the fullest with you," he answered and he grabbed my hand and we ran to the cotton candy booth. He dropped a dime in the man's hand and took a stick of pink cotton candy from the stand. He pulled the sticky cotton from the stick and fed it to me. I laughed as it got all over my face. Then we ran over to the photo booth. He popped a dime in the slot and before we were ready we had four pictures of us laughing. William put another dime in the slot. Four more flashes and we had pictures of us laughing and holding our teddy bears. Twenty cents later, eight photos revealed the intimate moments of us sharing our first real kiss. After that my heart and stomach were full of butterflies. I wanted to shout to the world and let everyone know how happy I was.

When we stepped out of the photo booth William made it official by taking my hands in his and asking, "Miss. Gwendolyn, the most beautiful daisy in the garden, would you make me the happiest man on this earth by being my girlfriend?"

I made him sweat a little bit as I made my thinking face. I pretended to look around and ponder the thought a bit. After about a minute I looked him right in his beautiful green eyes and said, "Most definitely."

After some whooping and hollering from him, we walked hand in hand to the shoreline. We sat on a bench and watched the seagulls swoop down in the water catching tiny fish. Once in a while, a ship's horn from out on the horizon would drown out the distant music coming from the band. A couple walked on the beach, hand in hand laughing and jumping as the waves washed over their bare feet. We just sat on the bench and took in every joyful thing that happened this evening. Then in the distance, we could hear the band play Ella Fitzgerald and Louis Armstrong's version of *Dream and Little Dream of Me*. As the singer belted out the first few words of the song, I stood up and pulled him off the bench. "Remember this song? This was our first slow song we danced to last night at the dance."

Darkness blanketed us as we swayed back and forth in each other's arms. Nothing else mattered at that moment. When the song ended his hand lifted up my chin. Our eyes met and then so did our lips again. My body became jelly in his arms and the butterflies in my stomach were all over the place.

"Do you promise to wait for me?" he whispered. I nodded my head as tears burned in my eyes. He took his hand and whipped them away as they rolled down my cheeks. Then he put his hand to his heart. "I love you Gwendolyn."

"I love you too William."

We walked hand in hand to the corner of my street. It was nearly nine o'clock. Neither of us wanted this night to end. He asked if we could meet up tomorrow. But unfortunately I had school and then I had to go straight to the library to work. He asked where the library was located and smiled when he realized it wasn't far from the base. He said he would try to stop by if he had liberty. Then he pulled a piece of paper with the ship's information on it.

"Promise you will write often."

"I promise I will." Then I wrapped my arms around his neck and pulled him to me. We laughed as we bumped heads but then we shared one last kiss under the stars. I tried laughing to hold back my tears, but they rushed down my cheeks.

"Dream a little dream of me," he sang softly in my ear. We held hands as we slowly walked in opposite directions. Holding tight until we couldn't hold anymore. He turned and waved then hugged his teddy bear. I did the same. When I got to the front steps I looked in his direction. He was still there watching me. He blew me a kiss and walked back to the base.

Chapter Five

The next day at school I couldn't focus on my studies. If the teacher would call on me I'd give an off the wall answer and I'd get reprimanded for being a distraction to the class. During our lunch break Sue-Ellen, Mary and Patricia swooned and giggled and admired me as I shared every detailed with them and showed them all the photo booth pictures.

After school, I had to go to the library. My heart ached. I wanted to see William one more time. Every time the little bell above the door dinged, I looked over to see if it was him. I was shelving the remaining books that I checked in about thirty minutes before I had to lock up. The rain started coming down hard. Lightning lit up the sky as thundered rolled heavy in the clouds. The outside looked like my heart felt. I started to cry. I pulled the teddy bear out of my bag and my tears soaked its fur.

The lights flickered as the building shook with a loud clap of thunder. I knew nobody would be coming to the library in weather like this, so I decided to close early. I grabbed my things and walked over to the door and stepped outside. I was getting my umbrella up and about to lock the library door when I saw a dark figure running towards me through the rain. I tried to open the door as fear overtook my body. The door always stuck when there was too much moisture in the air. I was about to run when the figure started calling my name,

"Daisy. Daisy, wait it's me." I recognized that voice. It was William. He ran right up under my umbrella and wrapped his arms around me, "I had to see you one last time before I fly out tomorrow. I didn't sleep last night because I couldn't stop thinking about you. All day today I couldn't focus because I was thinking about you."

I dropped my umbrella and we got soaked as we shared a kiss. As our bodies pushed up against the door, it gave way and opened and we stumbled back into the library. I locked the door as William took off his long black coat. The lightning cast shadows on the wall making it a little creepy inside. As William lead me over to a table, our shoes clicked on the tile floor drowning out the eerie silence. He turned on the little green light that was attached to the table. "Here I want you to have these," he said as he pulled a long silver chain out of his pocket. "These are called dog tags. I have to wear mine at all times ...in case something happens to me," he said slowly and quietly.

"We get several so I wanted to let you have one." He put it over my head and it hung perfectly on my chest. I think he noticed too because it was a minute before his eyes met mine. He cleared his throat as he took a piece of folded up paper and a handkerchief out of his pocket. "I wrote you your first letter. Don't read it now though. Wait until my airplane is gone okay." I nodded as he handed me the paper and the handkerchief. "I want you to have this. Just one more thing to remember me by. I sprayed some of my cologne on it so when you smell it, you think of me."

As I unfolded the handkerchief I saw blueberries and green vines stitched on it. "My mother embroidered the blueberries on it." William said, "She said it would remind me of home. Blueberries are my favorite. Mother grows blueberry bushes in the garden every year."

I smiled as I put the handkerchief up to my nose and inhaled. Then I dug around in my purse, "I didn't know if you'd stop by tonight. I was really hoping you would. I wrote you your first letter too." I said placing it in his hands. The rain pounded on the roof as thunder rolled across the dark sky. "But don't read it until you are out in the middle of that big blue damn ocean,." I said trying to hide my sadness.

He put the letter in his pocket. Then he lifted me up and sat me on the table. He stood in between my legs and we started kissing. More passionate than all the other times we've kissed. He started to gently kiss my neck sending goosebumps all over my body. When he started to unbutton my blouse I knew what was coming next. My heart pounded so loud I was sure William could hear it. As I started to unbutton his blue shirt I told him to carry me into the back supply room.

With the rain pounding down on the roof and lightning flashing through the window panes, amongst the tape and glue and all the books that needed to be mended, we consummated our love. That night was the first time for both of us.

I skipped school the next day and ran to the airfield to see William off. A giant airplane was being loaded with ammunition, crates of food, and other supplies and a few bags that said US Mail. All going over to resupply the sailors on the ships. Several sailors were lined up ready to board the massive airplane. There were so many family members crying and waving goodbye I knew William would never know I was there. A few of the families were holding giant pieces of paper with sayings on them like "I love you." and "Come home soon." I decided to ask someone if they had any extra paper. My heart skipped a beat when I was handed one with a big black marker. On the paper I wrote *Dream A Little Dream of Me*. Then I pulled the handkerchief out of my bag and let it fly in the wind as I held it tight with my paper. I only hoped he saw it as he was taking off.

Chapter Six

    I read William's letter every night before falling asleep. I prayed to the good lord to keep him safe and bring him home as soon as possible. I did my best to concentrate on my studies and on my duties at the library. I would get scared out of my mind when the principal of our school would come into the classroom with a solemn look on his face. It usually always meant he was there to tell a student their dad became the newest casualty of war. On the way home from school I would stop by the newspaper stand and read the latest headlines, hoping to read good news. But if I didn't see anything about the USS Essex then I figured that was good news.

About a month after William left I started getting sick. Sometimes I would get sick after eating something or from certain smells. And sometimes, it was for no reason at all. Sometimes I would ask to leave class and run down the hall to the bathroom, getting near the toilet just in time. But as soon as I finished throwing up, I felt better for the rest of the day. It wasn't until I realized I missed my period, that I understood why I was getting sick. I was pregnant. I didn't tell a soul. Not even Patricia, Sue-Ellen, or Mary. I only wrote about the pregnancy in the letters I sent to William, asking him what I should do. I was so scared. I was only seventeen. I knew Daddy would not be happy if he found out.

It was August when I stopped getting sick every day. But my clothes started to get tight around my waist. And of course, my mom noticed and she figured out my secret. She took me to the doctors to confirm her worst nightmare.

On the way home mom couldn't look at me. I saw her wipe away her tears several times. When we walked into the house she told me to sit on the couch. She would somehow break the news to my father. John and Patricia walked in the house as my father was stomping down the stairs, "Stay away from her Patricia or you may be next. Our little Daisy isn't so pure and innocent now is she?" He yelled right up in my face as tears started to pour down my cheeks. "Can't you see we can't afford another mouth to feed." he yelled with such anger in his voice my little siblings started to cry.

"Calm down Jimmy. Let's figure this out," mom said trying to keep calm.

"Calm down? Calm down? Lucille, if word gets out we are adding other mouth to this family people will think we have money. And when people think you have money they start asking you for things." He yelled pacing back and forth, "Hell, if we let her keep that baby, John and Patricia will think it is okay for them to have a baby. We will be the laughing stock of the town. Hell, worse yet, we will be shunned if anyone finds out our teenage daughter was knocked up. We'll have to move. No one can afford to move right now."

"Calm down Jimmy. You are scaring the children." Mom said losing her patients.

"For God Sakes woman stop telling me what to do." Dad yelled as he threw a small toy across the living room. Patricia, John, and I just sat there too scared to move.

My younger siblings still crying in fear of our dad. "I am calling that home for unwed mothers. What is the name of it?" Dad yelled in frustration, "Pine Meadows Asylum. And if you try and stop me ...so heaven help you woman." He yelled at my mom with his fist in the air. "Gwendolyn get your ass upstairs and start packing." he screamed as he picked up the phone.

I ran up the stairs with tears streaming down my face. Patricia was right behind me. "Gwendolyn, Gwendolyn what is going on? Are you pregnant?" I sat on my bed and just looked at her. One look and she knew the answer. "Is it William's?" she asked as she sat next to me and rubbed my back. But she already knew the answer. .

The following morning was dark and dismal with steady rain. Nobody spoke as mom got my younger siblings ready and dad packed my things in the trunk of the car. Patricia was no longer allowed over without adult supervision. John hugged me and kissed me on the head and said "Good Luck kiddo."

The three hour car ride to Pine Meadows Asylum was a silent three hour drive but felt more like eight hours. Mom and I cried most of the way. But you wouldn't notice because Mother Nature was still crying too.

It was about one o'clock in the afternoon when we pulled onto a gravel road full of potholes filled with rain water. In the distance, I could see a limestone building growing out of the ground as we drove closer. When we finally made it to the building I took a deep breath and stepped out of the car. The building was massive. The limestone was bright against the dark clouds but nonetheless uninviting. It stood three stories high with bars on the windows of the third floor. Vines climbed up the building covering some of the windows on the first floor. The bushes by the steps leading to the front door were almost bare and needed to be cut back. And what looked like what like an old flower bed, needed some major cleaning. A nurse, about thirty years old, opened the front door and waved at us. Mom gave me a hug and told me she loved me very much and told me to be brave. Mom took my bags out of the trunk as Dad signed some papers. Then he placed his hand on my shoulder and said, "Sorry it has to be this way," Then he and mom got back in the car. I watched as they drove slowly back down the gravel road. I wiped the tears from my eyes then made my way up the limestone steps, past the tall pillars and through the door and into the next journey of my life.

Chapter Seven

As I entered the building, I was quite surprised at how splendid the inside looked. The front part of the ceiling was arched with neat little designs in the molding. The tile floor was black and white and paintings, as you would find in an art museum, were hanging neatly on the walls. I could hear faint jazz music coming from somewhere in the distance. The music actually put me at ease as the nurse led me to the receptionist counter. She helped me fill out some paperwork and then put a plastic bracelet around my left wrist.

"What's this for?" I asked turning my wrist so I could read the writing on it.

"Oh, that's how we keep track of all our patients. It has your name and birthdate, your room number, and that symbol there tells us whether you need medication or not."

"Medication? I don't need medication." I protested.

"Oh, not now I agree. But we will see as time goes on. Now, follow me and listen closely to the rules as I give you a tour."

She led me past offices that belonged to the doctors. She told me I needed to sign in at the front desk ten minutes before my appointments and I better not be late. Next she took me by a storage room full of blankets, pillows, and hygiene products. She showed me the clipboard and the paper I am to fill out if I ever run out of anything. She showed me the laundry room and how to use the washer and dryer. She told me my laundry day was Tuesday and I better not forget because everyone has their own schedule and it cannot be messed up. I was also responsible for doing my own laundry right up until the baby came unless the doctor says otherwise. Next was a huge lounge. Windows took up most of the wall space which made it bright and inviting on a sunny day I'm sure. There were long tables for eating. She gave me the breakfast, lunch and dinner schedule. She advised me that the baby inside of me needs to eat so I better not miss a meal. Over in the far back two corners were couches, some chairs and a television. There was a little area with some toys, books, and paper and crayons. She told me some mothers who are sent here come with their children.

As we made our way to the second floor, the nurse told me I was to take the stairs at all times because the exercise was good for the baby. The elevators were only for patients who required a wheelchair. The second floor was made of cinder block walls painted a dark gray with ugly brown and tan tiles for the floors. Each door was numbered and had a tiny window for looking out and a slot long enough for a dinner tray to fit through. When asked about that, the nurse told me some mothers don't like to socialize.

We made our way to door fourteen. The nurse unlocked it and then handed me the key. I pushed the door open and looked inside. The walls and floors were exactly like the hallway. A small bed stood in the corner with sheets and blankets folded on the bed, ready for me to put on the mattress. A long dusty dresser with a cracked mirror sat in the opposite corner. And under a tiny window sat a writing desk and a lopsided chair. "This is your room now. Make yourself comfortable. You are going to be here for a few months."

"Why do the windows on the third floor have bars on them?" I asked quietly.

"The third floor is reserved for mothers and children who are sick with tuberculosis and for the mothers who aren't quite right in the head, if you know what I mean." And she shut the door and left me alone.

I didn't know what she meant and I hoped I never did. But I didn't have time to think about those mothers. I quickly got out my stationary and wrote a letter to William letting him know dad and mom found out about the pregnancy and I was sent to a home for unwed mothers. I told him about the tour the nurse gave me and about the rules I have to follow. I told him about the uninviting scenery and colors. I told him I loved and missed him and hoped he was staying safe.

I also wrote to Patricia and told her everything. I apologized to her as well. It was my fault she was no longer allowed at my house unless mom and dad were there. I also asked her to have John grab the mail every day before mom or dad got it. If there were any letters from William to please send them to me.

My first few weeks in the home went by slow. I was quick to get my schedule in order. The August weather was nice and hot so I would take time to walk around the unkempt grounds. I would sit and watch the little children play tag or kick a ball around. At night I would write letters to William, Patricia, and Mom. By the second week in September I was so depressed. I didn't even leave my room for two days. One day the nurse who brought my food and slid it through the slot, kept it open and quietly told me I had mail waiting at the receptionist's desk. You bet I was up and out of my room quicker than you could say elephants eat envelopes. I had three letters from Mom and Patricia. Each saying about the same thing. And there was a large manila envelope from John. Inside were two letters from William and one from John. John said dad was finally starting to cool off and there weren't any rumors going around about the pregnancy. He said that when he gets more letters from William he will be sure to send them to me. William's letters talked about his flight over to the USS Essex and about his duties on the ship. He wrote about getting seasick and that he loved me and our baby very much. Of course, I had to write to him and tell him I finally received his letters.

The letters didn't come as fast as I hoped they would. I'd get one a week or once every two weeks from Mom and Patricia. But they pretty much always said the same things. I even slowed my letters down as well. I'd send them each a letter once a week sometimes once every two weeks. One the first Monday in October I was the happiest I had been in a while. I received not one but two letters from William himself. He had received my letters about being sent to Pine Meadows Asylum. He apologized, saying it was his fault and when he came home we were going to get married. He had hoped I received his other letters even though he had sent them to my house. I, of course, had to write back right away telling him it wasn't his fault and yes I received them. I told him how I had asked John to grab the mail before mom and dad got it. And I couldn't wait until he came home so we could get married and raise our family. I also told him how big my belly was getting.

Chapter Eight

The first week in November I received two letters. The first one from Patricia. She told me she and John were coming to see me on Thanksgiving. I was so excited. I couldn't wait to see them. The second letter was from William. It was dated October 15, 1944. He said he was doing well but things are starting to get tense out in the Pacific. He told me he loved me and our baby and he missed me very much.

I tried to keep myself busy but the days dragged on. I couldn't wait to see John and Patricia. I learned how to sew and made myself a nice maternity dress to wear on Thanksgiving. And I was on the finishing stages of a patchwork quilt. I even had enough energy to babysit a couple of small children so one of the moms could have a break. The nurses and my doctor even noticed a change in my mood.

I was up bright and early on Thanksgiving morning pacing back and forth in front of my small little window waiting for John and Patricia to arrive. The cooks had been busy in the kitchen preparing a huge Thanksgiving meal for all the families that were coming today. There was even a small craft table for the little children to color paper Native American feathers and make a headdress. I became bored of waiting I decided to go join the little ones. Soon afterward someone tapped on my shoulder. When I turned around I saw John and Patricia. I hugged them both as best I could with my big belly.

"AHHHH!" I screamed excitedly, "I missed you both so much."

"Hey, kiddo how are?" John said hugging me again.

"Oh, Daisy you look so beautiful." Patricia said grabbing my hands, "How do you feel?'

"I have been feeling wonderful ever since I received your letter saying you were coming for Thanksgiving."

I gave them a tour of the building and introduced them to some of the other moms and their children. For lunch there was turkey, mashed potatoes, gravy, dressing and desserts galore. It smelled so wonderful and tasted even better. The baby started to kick while we ate. I grabbed Patricia's hand and placed it on my stomach so she could feel it.

After lunch, we went back to my room so we could have some private family time.

"How come Mom and Dad didn't come with you guys? I was really hoping Mom would surprise me." I said as I made myself comfortable in the rocking chair.

John replied, "Mom and Dad and the kids drove up to Wisconsin to visit Dad's brother. His brother says the economy is doing really well there despite the war. So dad wanted to go check it out for himself."

"John and I have some news to share with you," Patricia said with excitement in her voice. She pulled something out of her pocket and placed it on her finger. Then she waved her hand in front of me, "We're getting married." She squealed. "But don't tell anybody yet. John just proposed to me last night, so you're the first to know."

"Oh my goodness." I said grabbing her hand gazing at the ring. "Congratulations guys." And I got up and hugged them both.

We visited until I was ready to take a nap. They hugged me goodbye and promised to give Dad and Mom and all the little ones back home big hugs from me. I was as happy as a little kid on Christmas as I waved goodbye and watched them drive down the gravel road.

Two days later on November 25, 1944 my life changed forever. Everyone was gathered around both televisions when I came down to the lounge area. Images of smoke billowing out of a ship showed on the screen. The reporter came on and said a Japanese kamikaze plane had crashed into the USS Essex and there were casualties. Everything around me became blurry, my head started to spin, and I fell to my knees. I don't remember much after that. I just remember waking up in the hospital wing of the building with an IV in my arm and a cool rag on my forehead.

A nurse noticed I was coming too, "Hey honey how are you feeling? Are you okay?"

"Where am I?" I asked realizing I had things attached to me.

"It's okay honey. I'll run and grab Dr. Flagstone. You just lay still."

"Where's William," I asked, but the nurse was already out in the hall.

Soon Dr. Flagstone came in. He grabbed a clipboard off of the foot of the bed I was in and looked over the papers that were on it. Then he flicked the IV bag that hung near my head and took my pulse. "Everything seems to be okay. How are you feeling Gwendolyn?"

"Where's William? I need to know if William is okay." I said in a panic.

"Who's William?" The doctor asked confused.

"William. The Father of my baby. He's on the USS Essex. I need to know if he is okay." I cried.

"Oh sweetie." the nurse said as she came to my side. "The news reporters don't know much right now. Give it some time and we will hear something. I'm sure he is alright. In the meantime, take this medicine. It will help you sleep."

"I don't want medicine," I screamed. "I want William. My baby needs a father."

I was eventually released from the hospital wing and allowed to go back to my room. But instead, I spent most of the time in front of the television watching the news reports praying for good news about William. But over and over this was all I heard:

"The USS Essex was struck by a Japanese Kamikaze plane off the Philippine Islands. Sixteen members on board were killed. Forty-Four seriously wounded. I prayed William was one of the ones that was safe or injured.

However, after that day I never received any more letters from him.

Chapter Nine

In the early hours of December 15, 1944, I woke up screaming in terrible pain. I got out of bed and tried to walk down the hall to get the nurse on duty but I was sopping wet. All I could do was scream in pain. Luckily a nurse came to my beck and call and saw that my water had broken. I was in labor. She got me in a wheelchair and rushed me back to the hospital wing.

I laid in bed for hours screaming in agonizing pain as my stomach and my butt muscles contracted. The doctor and nurses would come in and check on me and stick their fingers up inside me. Then they'd tell me I was doing a great job. A great job doing what? Screaming? I thought. Finally about ten o'clock that morning they told me I could push.

So I pushed and pushed and pushed. Finally, the pain went away and they placed a baby girl upon my chest. Oh, she was so beautiful and so tiny with a squeaky little cry and blue eyes with a little speck of green. I just had a feeling her eyes would be green when she grew older, just like her daddy's. For the first time in a long, long time, I was crying happy tears.

"What are you going to name her?" the nurse asked me as she helped me get her situated so I could fill out her birth certificate.

"Wilma Gwendolyn-Daisy Barret," I said with a smile.

"My, that is quite a name," the nurse replied.

"Wilma is for her daddy's name, William, in memory of him." I answered as I gazed into her beautiful newborn eyes. "She even has his skin tone."

"That's nice." the nurse replied as if she didn't really care. She was too focused on painting Wilma's tiny foot with ink then pressed it up against her birth certificate. After they cleaned off her little foot the nurse took her from my arms and wrapped up in a tiny blanket and walked out of the room with her.

Another nurse came in shortly afterward and had me sign some paperwork for Wilma. When we were finished, I asked, "Where did the other nurse take my baby? Will she be back soon?"

"Oh honey." the nurse said with a pitiful expression. "You're only seventeen. You can't raise a child by yourself. When you came to us in August, your parents signed papers to have the baby put up for adoption."

My heart instantly broke. I had never in my life felt so betrayed, so angry, so hurt, and so empty. My tears stained the very last word in the letter I wrote to William, in hopes that he may be still alive. I told him I was forced to give up our daughter, Wilma Gwendolyn-Daisy Barret. I told him how beautiful she was and how I saw a speck of green in her newborn baby blue eyes. I signed the letter with the words, "I love you forever, in heaven Dream A Little Dream of Me. Gwendolyn, the most beautiful flower in the garden."

Chapter Ten

    "Oh, Grandma Daisy!" I exclaimed as I wiped the tears from my eyes," I'm so sorry. You lost everything that meant so much to you in such a short time." I said as I hugged her.

    "It's okay child. Things in life happen. But I have you, don't I? And you mean the world to me." She replied as she hugged me back.

    "Grandma Daisy, do you think Wilma was adopted to a good family? Do you think she is still alive?"

    Grandma shook her head, "No child. Tuberculosis was a horrible illness back then. It affected infants and the elderly.

Even healthy people could contract Tuberculosis. Being in such tight quarters as I was with those women in that home, illnesses would spread quickly. Same as it did in the orphanage where they took Wilma. A cure wasn't found for Tuberculosis until the end of the war. Most who had TB as it's called now, died. She is in heaven with her daddy William."

"Did you get to go back home with Great Grandma Lucille and Great Grandpa Jimmy?"

Grandma sighed, "Well on Christmas day Mom, Dad, John, and the younger siblings picked me up from the home. They had a small trailer hitched to the back of the car. Mom tried to hug me but I wouldn't hug back. I didn't even look her or dad in the eye. I was so angry at her and Daddy. To make matters even worse, when I got in the car, John told me Daddy sold the house and we were moving to Wisconsin near Dad's brother. I asked about the whereabouts of Patricia. John told me her dad called off the engagement on account that he didn't want his daughter moving across the country. And my dad wouldn't let John stay in California. Then John just stared out the car window as we made that bumpy trip down the gravel road away from Pine Meadows Asylum. It was a long and quite drive to our new life in Wisconsin.

Life wasn't the same in Wisconsin. Dad had a job lined up, but it didn't last long. Money was extremely tight. Dad and Mom fought a lot and Dad took to drinking. He would go out drinking and come home late at night. I remember waking up in the morning and seeing Mom trying to cover up her black eye with makeup.

John would find himself in bad situations. Sometimes I'd hear him leave late at night and then he wouldn't come home for three or four days. More than once I remember going to the jail house with bail money for him. My heart ached for John. Not only was he my older brother, but he was my best friend. Or he used to be anyway. The move to Wisconsin changed our relationship too.

I went to school just to get out of the house. But there were times when I didn't feel like going to school. I'd just stayed locked in my room and sleep for the whole day. Dad was too busy drinking, and Mom was too busy trying to make him happy and my younger siblings behave and stay quiet so dad wouldn't get mad and hit them. So nobody noticed I was skipping school.

But then the snow started to melt and the flowers and trees bloomed and I saw how pretty our new Wisconsin town was. I just couldn't stay inside. There was a big field by the school. Boys would go there to play football after school and on the weekends. I started going and sitting on the slope of the hill away from the other girls that were there just giggling away. I actually went in the hopes that maybe I'd see John there. But he never was. The boys would play football until sunset on school days and all day long on the weekend.

Then, on my eighteenth birthday, about sunset, the game paused and the boys started walking home in all directions. I was getting up from the ground and was about to walk up the hill when I dropped one of my school books. I turned to pick it up but one of the boys had gotten to it first. I couldn't help but notice he was a little older than all the other boys who were playing football. He was so handsome and his smile just melted my heart when he handed me my book. He ended up walking me home. He told me he was just about to graduate from the college down the street with a degree in finance. He was going to work with his dad who owned the bank in town. Of course, mom and dad threw a fit when they saw me walk up the sidewalk with this boy. They absolutely forbade me to see him ever again. They didn't want their young daughter to get pregnant again. So Harold and I had to keep our new relationship a secret. He was so sweet and kind to me and so funny. And when he looked me in the eyes, I noticed his twinkled like William's eyes did. Being with Harold made me feel like I still had a small piece of William with me. He would say the same thing William use to say about my name, "Gwendolyn, the most beautiful daisy in the garden." Even sneaking around with him made me want to be with him even more.

On the night of his college graduation, he proposed to me. I, of course, said yes. With all the excitement, one thing lead to another and we slept together. But in our eyes, it was okay because we were engaged. I ran home the next morning and snuck into my room via the big oak tree outside my window. If mom or dad found out I stayed the night with Harold, I'm sure they would have sent me away again. When I got inside my room I saw a note laying on my pillow. It was from John. He said he was tired of getting in trouble. He felt like if he stayed he would turn into our father, a drunk. He still loved Patricia and was going back to California to be with her. He asked me not to say anything to mom and dad for a least a week or two. In my heart I made that promise to my brother. It looked like things were looking up for the both of us.

In June I started to get sick again. That's when I told Harold about William and Wilma. He told me we needed to get married right away. We used his first paycheck from the bank to get me a wedding dress. With his second paycheck we would get a small apartment in town. On Saturday July 7th, 1945 Harold and I were married in the court house. Harold was in a nice black tuxedo and I in a white lace wedding dress. The night before the wedding was the last time I saw my dad. He went to a bar and never came home. Rumors circulated for a few months about the things that had happened to him. But with a baby on the way, Harold and I had more important things to worry about. My mom supported us with as much praise as she could. But now she was a single mom still raising three young children, so she couldn't help us financially.

Then I remember like it happened yesterday. It was Thursday, February 14th, 1946, Valentine's Day. We had just sat down to eat supper when I started having horrible stomach pains. Harold called the doctor and we rushed to the hospital. Your mom was born that night. She was so beautiful. She had a head full of hair, blue eyes and the cutest little squeaky cry, that made Harold laugh so hard.

"Wait a minute Grandma Daisy." I interrupted, "Harold is my grandpa? I thought Grandpa's name was Harry?"

"Yes, Harold is your Grandpa. Everyone just called him Harry." Grandma Daisy replied with a laugh.

I sat quiet for a moment to take in everything I had just learned about my grandma and her life growing up, then asked, "Grandma Daisy, if William was your first true love and you loved him with all your heart, how can you also love Grandpa with all your heart?"

"Oh child," she said as she took my hand in hers, "Love is a beautiful yet complicated thing. There are many different ways to love people. I suspect in the next couple of years you will start to understand."

Chapter Eleven

Grandma Daisy passed away on a Tuesday. Only three short months after moving in with us. Mom let me take a week off from school to see my aunts, uncles and cousins who were in town for the funeral. Sunday night I stayed up all night doing my project on World War Two for History class. I tried holding back my tears as I glued the photo booth pictures of Grandma Daisy and William on my poster.

On Monday we were able to display our posters in the school library and we all took turns giving our presentation. My friends and I were walking around looking at all the displays when I noticed something. A picture. A picture of a Navy sailor. I had seen that sailor before. I got my eye balls right next to that poster and stared at the picture until I knew in my heart I knew that sailor.

McKenzie was new at our school. She had just started at my school a week before my grandma had died so I didn't really get a chance to introduce myself or get to know her. "How did you get a hold of my picture?" I asked her in a mean tone.

"What are you talking about?" McKenzie replied confused.

"This picture right here. This picture of the Navy sailor. You took that from my collection of pictures my grandma gave me."

"I don't even know what picture collection you are talking about. This is my grandfather." she tried speaking in a calm tone.

But I was getting frustrated. I ran over to my poster and pulled off a picture of William Barret in his naval uniform and showed it to McKenzie. "See. It's the same person. This is William Barret. I have several pictures of him. You stole this picture from my collection." I yelled.

Our teacher came over and tried to get things between McKenzie and I figured out. We ended up down in the Principal's office. I was so irate he couldn't understand what was going on, so he ended up calling mine and McKenzie's mom. .

"Please have a seat Mrs. Jenkins and Mrs. Cartwright." The principal motioned to the chairs as our moms walked in. "Mrs. Cartwright, it seems as though Hanna feels McKenzie stole a picture from her." He handed my mom the picture in question. "Can you make any sense out of this?"

My mom looked at the picture and sighed, "Before Hanna's grandma, my mom, passed away she was helping her grandma go through some old things in the attic. They came across an envelope of pictures and letters. Among them were pictures and letters from a sailor my mom had met, his name was William Barret. This is him." Then my mom looked at McKenzie and politely asked "Sweetie how did you get my daughter's picture."

McKenzie looked nervous. But before she could say anything her mom interjected, "Mrs. Cartwright, I'm sorry for this confusion, but this is McKenzie's grandfather."

"Please, call me Helen." My mom replied as she held her hand out for Mrs. Jenkins to shake.

"I'm Wilma. Pleasure to meet you."

"HOLD THE PHONE!" I yelled excitedly as everybody in the principal's office looked at me.

"What did you say your name was?"

Mrs. Jenkins looked at my mother with confusion in her eyes then answered, "Wilma?"

"Oh my goodness." excitement obvious in my voice, "Were you born in California on December 15th, 1944?"

Again Mrs. Jenkins looked at my mom with confusion then asked, "Helen, how did your daughter get my information?" she asked in almost an angry tone.

"Just please answer my question Mrs. Jenkins." I begged, "Were you born in California on December 15th, 1944?"

"Yes. Yes, I was."

"And were you adopted?"

"Hanna!" my mom yelled, "Now you are getting to personal young lady."

"Please Mrs. Jenkins. Please. I'm sorry. But if you answer the way I hope you do then I will explain everything." I pleaded.

"Yes I was adopted. My father William Barret told me he fell in love with a girl before he shipped out and she got pregnant and her parents made her put the baby, which was me, up for adoption. The girl wrote to William to explain everything. My father was discharged from the Navy because of injuries he received when a plane crashed into his ship out in the Pacific. He went around to every orphanage in California to find me."

"You're right Mrs. Jenkins. You're right." I screamed jumping up and down with joy. "Grandma Daisy named you Wilma after your daddy William, in memory of him. Grandma Daisy thought he died because she saw the plane crash on the television when she was at the home for unwed mothers. Mom. Mom. This is your sister. "I yelled in a happy tone as I hugged my mom.

Both women and the principal looked confused, even McKenzie. "Um Wilma, I apologize. I have no idea what my daughter is talking about."

"Mom, Grandma never told you about Wilma because life became busy for her and grandpa after you were born. She just assumed Wilma, like a lot of newborns, died of Tuberculosis, especially those who were in orphanages. I have a copy of Wilma's birth certificate in the envelope with all the letters grandma gave me."

Everyone was quiet for a few minutes and just stared at me. Then finally my mom cleared her throat and said, "Um Wilma, would you like to come over for tea and we can get all this straightened out? Wilma smiled, "I would love to.

Chapter Twelve

Wilma came over for tea that afternoon. I begged my mom to let me have tea with them, but Mom said they needed adult time in order to get everything straightened out first. So naturally, I sat in the dining room, out of sight, and listened to Wilma's side of the story and the memories of her childhood she told my mom. I also learned that William had passed away only a short time before my grandma. It was comforting to know that both of the men my grandma loved so dearly, were waiting for her at those pearly gates.

It was almost time for supper when she and Mom hugged and said goodbye. I was on Mom's heels begging for Wilma to stay so I could talk with her. Mom assured me there would soon be a chance for me to share the story Grandma Daisy told me. Mom fixed fish sticks and french fries and sliced apples for dinner for Hattie and me and told us we could eat our supper in the living room while watching television. Mom never lets us eat in the living room. So I knew she and Dad were having a conversation about the events that transpired this afternoon.

The next day at school, Mckenzie and I became fast friends and told everyone we were actually long lost cousins. She told me she moved from Ephraim, Wisconsin which is only about two hundred and thirty miles from my small town. She and her family had moved here for a job offer her dad had accepted. Now we only live three streets down from one another. And to think, Grandma Daisy lived only about two hundred and thirty miles south of William and her daughter Wilma. The daughter Grandma Daisy was forced to give up for adoption. The daughter whom she thought had died from tuberculosis.

Mom and Wilma spent every day together for next week and a half getting to know one another. Mom also spent a lot of time on the phone telling my aunts and uncles about Wilma. So I was not surprised when our house was full of family on Thanksgiving Day. As Mom introduced Wilma and her husband, my new Uncle Francis, to all the adults, I introduced McKenzie and her younger brother, Billy, to all their new cousins. And if all this excitement wasn't enough for the family, my great Uncle John and Aunt Patricia surprised us all, when we saw them both walking up to our front porch, thanks to the help of their five children and several grandchildren. When Uncle John moved back to California, he and Patricia had married. After several years of trying to have children, they decided to adopt. Within a three year span, they adopted five children. After a few years in California, they decided to move to Wisconsin to be closer to Grandma Daisy and her family.

It was a good thing Mom asked a few of the relatives to bring card tables and chairs. People sat and ate Thanksgiving dinner in the kitchen, in the dining room, in the living room and even out on the back three season's porch. It made my heart beat with joy as I watched all of my family accept Wilma and her family as part of our family. I knew for a fact, Grandma Daisy, Grandpa Harry, and even William were smiling up in heaven as they were looking down on us. My family truly had a lot to be thankful for. I couldn't help but think what it would be like had I not noticed McKenzie's picture of William that day in the library.

Finally, the time had come that I had been waiting for since the day I had realized who Wilma was in the Principal's office. After everyone had finished eating and leftovers were put in Tupperware, and the dishes had been washed, Mom announced that everyone should try to squeeze into the living room. Everyone made themselves comfortable on the couch, on folding chairs, and on the steps leading upstairs. Some even gathered in the archway of the dining room and the doorway of the front porch. My little cousins sat on the laps of their parents' and on the floor. Finally my moment was here. Butterflies filled my stomach and my palms began to sweat. I could hear my heartbeat in my chest as everyone quietly focused on me. I took a few deep breaths before I began my speech.

"Looking at all of you this evening, I can tell we are a very blessed family. If it weren't for

Grandpa Harry, Grandma Daisy, and William Barret, we wouldn't be celebrating Thanksgiving together at my house. Like last year and the years prior, we would celebrate Thanksgiving with our immediate families. We all can admit the last six months have been a roller coaster of emotions. Putting Grandma Daisy's house up for sale, getting it cleaned out, dividing her things between all of us, and finding a home for her was extremely stressful at times. We all knew her health was not the greatest, but we were all shocked and heartbroken when she passed away. "I paused to take a deep breath. Everyone was still silent and smiling at me.

"The day before Grandma Daisy moved into our house, Hattie and I were helping her clean out her attic. In an old trunk, we found her wedding dress she wore when she and Grandpa Harry were married. In that same trunk, I found these pictures and letters," I unfolded the cloth handkerchief with the embroidered blueberries on it and showed everyone the photo booth pictures and letters Grandma Daisy and William had written to each other while they were apart.

"We all know how horrible World War II was and the hardships families faced and the unbelievably horrible things soldiers and sailors saw - things that most won't speak about. It was also a time of romance. People falling in love, only to be separated by deployments. Letters were written with the most heartfelt feelings. And those who were lucky enough had the most wonderful end of war homecoming celebrations. Well, Grandma Daisy's romantic war story started in April of 1944."

It was easy for me to be my theatrical self when I first told of Grandma Daisy and William at the dance and at the fair. I noticed my family smiling, nodding their heads, and even laughing. But when I got to the part when Great Grandpa Jimmy sent her away to Pine Meadows Asylum, something overtook me and tears started welling up in my eyes. I paused and took a couple of breaths. I looked out to the crowd and found Wilma. I nodded to her as tears rolled down my blushing cheeks. She stood up and came over to me. She gave me a big hug and held my hand. Then she continued with the story.

There wasn't a dry eye in my house when Wilma had finished our story. We all sat in silence for a few minutes taking in all we heard. When the silence started to get uncomfortable for me, I began to pass the letters and pictures around while Dad put on another pot of coffee. As everyone quietly chatted about their memories of Grandma Daisy, Grandpa Harry, and William, I sneaked off to Dad's den. I went through the old records he and Mom had received from Grandma. I found the record single I was looking for. I placed it on the turntable of the record player and turned the volume up to a comfortable level so all could hear.

Ella Fitzgerald's pure and vibrant voice brought a youthful feeling to the room as she and Louis Armstrong sang *Dream a Little Dream of Me.* Sitting on the steps, I absentmindedly took the handkerchief out of my sweatshirt pocket and started to sniff it. Years in the attic trunk made it smell all musty. But I swear I could smell a faint smell of a cologne. I closed my eyes and pictured Grandma Daisy and William Barret slow dancing together on the beach the night of the fair. I pictured them walking hand in hand laughing at the conversations they shared. And though Grandma Daisy never did know if William saw her standing there watching his plane take off, I know in my heart he saw her and blew a million kisses to her as he ascended into the sky.

Grandma Daisy was right about daisies being strong rooted and producing new daisy patches every year. Our family just became bigger because of Wilma and her family. And though Grandma Daisy had so much heartache in her young life, she was the strongest woman I knew and raised the best family in the world...My family

The End

Author's notes

This story and characters are fictional. World War II, the Kamikaze plane that crashed into the USS Essex, and tuberculosis are very much real. Most of the countries in the world were active in WWII which lasted from 1939-1945. Adolf Hitler wanted world power. His army built several concentration camps in Europe which held people of the Jewish religion and decent, ultimately killing them with gas, starvation, and or shooting them at point blank range.

Japan was an ally to Germany. Most of their battles took place in the Pacific Ocean. Japan's fighting tactic was using Kamikaze planes. The Japanese pilots took the oath and ultimately knew they would die as they crashed their planes into naval ships. Several ships were destroyed. One being the USS Essex.

On November 25, 1944 a Kamikaze plane exploded when it crashed onto the flight deck of the USS Essex near the Philippine Islands in the Pacific Ocean. Sixteen men were killed and forty-four were seriously injured.

By the end of WWII more than 40,000,000 military servicemen and civilians were killed. This was the bloodiest conflict and largest war in world history.

Tuberculosis is still around today. It is a disease caused by a bacteria that mainly affects the lungs. When untreated, a person with tuberculosis can spread the disease by coughing or sneezing. In the 1920's it was the leading cause of death in children ages 1-4 years old. During WWII tuberculosis spread quickly do to overcrowding in hospitals, orphanages, and economically poor cities and small towns. Anti-tuberculosis drugs were invented near the end of the war.

On a happier note, everything Grandma Daisy's character said about the flower daisies is true. Daisies are also the world's largest plant family. They are found every in the world except Antarctica. And they have a lot of medicinal properties. They are also my favorite flower, which is why I chose to incorporate them into my story.

Bibliography

Life and Death Aboard the U.S.S. Essex
By: Richard W. Streb
Dorrance Publishing, 1999
http://www.kamikazeimages.net/books/ships/
streb/index.htm

The Holocaust Encyclopedia
World War II in the Pacific
https://encyclopedia.ushmm.org/content/en/ar
ticle/world-war-ii-in-the-pacific

Tuberculosis
Reviewed by: Nicole A. Green MD
https://kidshealth.org/en/teens/tuberculosis.h
tml

10 Things You Didn't Know About Daisies
By Andy Bloxham, August 4th, 2015
https://www.telegraph.co.uk/gardening/84819
65/Top-10-facts-about-daisies.html

About the Author

Heather lives in a small town in Wisconsin with her husband of almost twenty years, two kids and several pets. She married her husband shortly out of high school and they spent fourteen years in the Navy. Heather loved being a Navy wife and said she would do it all over again. She now works in the library at the local middle school. Her favorite book genre is historical fiction. Heather's favorite flower is the daisy. She hopes you might pick up on some of the irony in the story. This is also Heather's first book.

Made in the USA
Lexington, KY
23 July 2019